W9-AUH-862

One day I decided to buy a pet.
I emptied out my piggy bank.
I had one quarter, two dimes, two nickels,
and eight pennies.

I ran to the pet store
and looked at the puppies.
They were little fur balls jumping around.
There was one that licked my hand,
but he was ten dollars.

So I went to look at the kittens.
They all smiled at me.
But they were five dollars.

I counted my money again
and went over to the canaries.
They sat on their perches
and sang.
But they were three dollars.

The fish bubbling in the tank were two dollars.

I didn't even have
enough money
for a turtle on a rock.

The only thing in the store I could buy
was a dog leash.
So I bought one.

I said good-bye and walked out
of the store.

As I walked down the street,
I began to pretend there
was a puppy
at the end of my leash.

He was furry and small
and did everything I said.

He didn't chase cats.
He didn't growl.
And he was very clean.

When I got home, I fed him.
He didn't eat much at all.

After dinner we went for a walk.
I was so proud. Everyone looked at us.

Then we played in the backyard
till it was time for bed.

I gave him my pillow
and he went
right to sleep.

I dreamed about my puppy all night.
I taught him how to stay, roll over,
and jump fences.
He learned everything right away.

The next day I took him to school.
To show and tell.

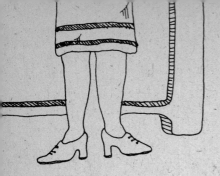

The teacher said he was
so good he could stay
in the classroom all day.

At recess all the kids
came over to play with him.
Except for Freddy Snarf.
I don't like Freddy Snarf.

On the way home from school
we saw a poster.
It said,
"Dog show Saturday,
May sixteenth."

So I took my puppy right home
and gave him a bath

and shined him.

And on Saturday
we were ready.

Everyone looked at us

when we came in.

The judges came over and I told them
all about my puppy.
They had a conference.

Then the contest started.
My puppy did everything perfectly.
He stayed when I said "stay"
and he walked right beside me.

But the first prize
went to a beautiful poodle.

The second prize
went to a big collie.

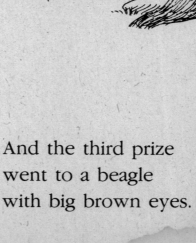

And the third prize
went to a beagle
with big brown eyes.

Then the judges came over to me
and handed me a special prize.
They pinned a ribbon on the leash
and gave me a card that said,
"This coupon entitles the bearer
to one puppy at the pet store."

I thanked them and ran out
of the dog show
all the way to the pet store

where I got

another puppy.